AF556122

Aarti Sangrah

The Complete Aarti Sangrah with English Transliterations

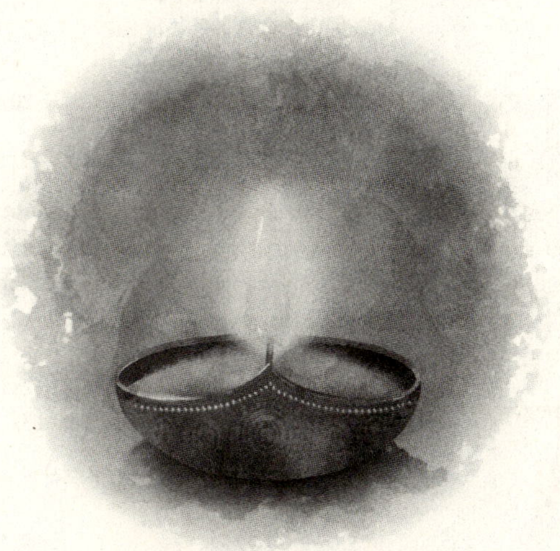

Published in Sanskriti Press
Rupa Publications India Pvt. Ltd 2025
161-B/4, Gulmohar House,
Yusuf Sarai Community Centre,
New Delhi 110049

Sales centres:
Bengaluru Chennai
Hyderabad Kolkata Mumbai

P-ISBN: 978-93-7003-763-2
E-ISBN: 978-93-7003-222-4

First impression 2025

10 9 8 7 6 5 4 3 2 1

Printed in India

Contents

परिचय

संस्कृति प्रेस में, हमारा उद्देश्य भारत की समृद्ध आध्यात्मिक परंपराओं का संरक्षण और उत्सव मनाना है, ताकि पवित्र ग्रंथों को भक्तों के हृदयों के और करीब लाया जा सके। हमें यह प्रस्तुत करते हुए अत्यंत खुशी हो रही है- 'आरती संग्रह', जो सबसे प्रतिष्ठित हिंदू देवताओं को समर्पित आरतियों का एक व्यापक संग्रह है। यह द्विभाषी संस्करण, जिसमें आरतियां हिंदी और रोमन लिपि में उपलब्ध हैं, भक्तों को उनकी आध्यात्मिक जड़ों से जोड़ने और भक्ति को प्रेरित करने के उद्देश्य से तैयार किया गया है।

आरती, हिंदू पूजा का एक अभिन्न हिस्सा हैं, जो भक्तिपूर्ण भजनों के माध्यम से देवताओं की महिमा का गान करती हैं और उनके आशीर्वाद का आह्वान करती हैं। यह संग्रह प्रमुख देवताओं और देवियों की आरतियों को सम्मिलित करता है, जो हिंदू आध्यात्मिकता के विविध पहलुओं को समेटे हुए है। बाधाओं को दूर करने वाले भगवान गणेश से लेकर सृष्टि के संरक्षक भगवान विष्णु तक; करुणामयी माता दुर्गा से लेकर उदार अन्नपूर्णा देवी तक, यह पुस्तक हर अवसर और उद्देश्य के लिए भक्ति के सार को समेटती है।

इन आत्मीय भजनों के माध्यम से, 'आरती संग्रह' दिव्यता का उत्सव मनाता है और दैनिक प्रार्थना, त्योहारों और व्यक्तिगत पूजा के लिए एक अमूल्य मार्गदर्शिका प्रदान करता है। चाहे आप पारंपरिक लिपि से परिचित हों या रोमन लिपि में पाठ करना पसंद करें, यह संस्करण भक्तों को सहजता और भक्ति के साथ पाठ करने की सुविधा प्रदान करता है।

हम, संस्कृति प्रेस में, इस पवित्र संग्रह को आपके समक्ष प्रस्तुत करने का गौरव अनुभव करते हैं और आशा करते हैं कि यह आपके आध्यात्मिक पथ को समृद्ध करेगा। दिव्य प्रकाश आपका मार्गदर्शन करे और ये आरतियां आपके जीवन में शांति, सुख और आशीर्वाद लेकर आएं।

**"दिव्य भजनों की मधुरता से
अपनी भक्ति को प्रेरित करें!"**

Introduction

At Sanskriti Press, our mission is to preserve and celebrate India's rich spiritual traditions by bringing sacred texts closer to the hearts of devotees. We are delighted to present *Aarti Sangrah*, a comprehensive collection of Aartis dedicated to the most revered Hindu deities. Designed to inspire devotion and connect readers with their spiritual roots, this bilingual edition features the Aartis in both Hindi and Roman script, making it accessible to a wider audience.

Aartis are an integral part of Hindu worship, expressing devotion through melodic hymns that glorify the deities and invite their blessings. This collection includes Aartis for prominent gods and goddesses, encompassing diverse aspects of Hindu spirituality. From the remover of obstacles, Lord Ganesha, to the supreme preserver, Lord Vishnu; from the compassionate Mother Durga to the bountiful Annapurna Devi, this book captures the essence of devotion for every occasion and purpose.

Through these soulful hymns, *Aarti Sangrah* celebrates the divine and provides an invaluable guide for daily prayers, festive occasions, and personal devotion. Whether you are familiar with the traditional script or prefer Roman transliterations, this edition allows devotees to chant with ease and devotion.

We at Sanskriti Press are honored to bring this sacred compilation to you and hope it enriches your spiritual journey. May the divine light guide you, and may these Aartis bring peace, happiness, and blessings into your life.

Let the divine melodies inspire your devotion!

श्री गणेश जी की आरती

जय गणेश जय गणेश जय गणेश देवा
माता जाकी पार्वती पिता महादेवा ।। जय ...
एक दंत दयावंत चार भुजा धारी ।।
माथे सिंदूर सोहे मूसे की सवारी ।। जय ...
अंधन को आंख देत, कोढ़िन को काया ।।
बांझन को पुत्र देत, निर्धन को माया ।। जय ...
पान चढ़े फूल चढ़े और चढ़े मेवा ।
लड्डुअन का भोग लगे संत करें सेवा ।। जय ...
'सूर' श्याम शरण आए सफल कीजे सेवा
जय गणेश जय गणेश जय गणेश देवा ।। जय ...

Shri Ganesh Ji Ki Aarti

Jai Ganesh Jai Ganesh Jai Ganesh Deva
Mata Jaaki Parvati Pita Mahadeva II Jai ...
Ek Dant Dayavant Chaar Bhuja Dhaari
Maathe Sindoor Sohe Moose Ki Sawari II Jai ...
Andhan Ko Aankh Det, Kodhin Ko Kaaya
Baanjhan Ko Putra Det, Nirdhan Ko Maya II Jai ...
Paan Chadhe Phool Chadhe Aur Chadhe Meva
Ladduan Ka Bhog Lage Sant Karein Seva II Jai ...
'Soor' Shyam Sharan Aaye Safal Kijiye Seva
Jai Ganesh Jai Ganesh Jai Ganesh Deva II Jai ...

श्री हरि विष्णु जी की आरती

ॐ जय जगदीश हरे, प्रभु! जय जगदीश हरे।
भक्तजनों के संकट, क्षण में दूर करे॥
ॐ जय जगदीश हरे

जो ध्यावै फल पावै, दुःख बिनसै मनका।
सुख सम्पत्ति घर आवै, कष्ट मिटै तनका॥
ॐ जय जगदीश हरे

मात-पिता तुम मेरे, शरण गहूँ किसकी।
तुम बिन और न दूजा, आस करूँ जिसकी॥
ॐ जय जगदीश हरे

तुम पूरन परमात्मा, तुम अंतर्यामी।
पार ब्रह्म परमेश्वर, तुम सबके स्वामी॥
ॐ जय जगदीश हरे

तुम करुणा के सागर, तुम पालनकर्ता।
मैं मूरख खल कामी, कृपा करो भर्ता॥
ॐ जय जगदीश हरे

तुम हो एक अगोचर, सबके प्राणपति।
किस विधि मिलूँ दयामय, तुमको मैं कुमती ।।
ॐ जय जगदीश हरे

दीनबन्धु, दुःखहर्ता तुम ठाकुर मेरे।
अपने हाथ उठाओ, द्वार पड़ा तेरे ।।
ॐ जय जगदीश हरे

विषय विकार मिटाओ, पाप हरो देवा।
श्रद्धा-भक्ति बढ़ाओ, संतन की सेवा ।।
ॐ जय जगदीश हरे

Shri Hari Vishnu Ji Ki Aarti

Om Jai Jagdish Hare, Prabhu! Jai Jagdish Hare ।
Bhaktajanon Ke Sankat, kshan Mein Door Kare ॥
Om Jai Jagdish Hare

Jo Dhyavein Phal Paavein, Dukh Binsai Manka ।
Sukh Sampatti Ghar Aavein, Kasht Mitaai Tankaa ॥
Om Jai Jagdish Hare

Maat-Pita Tum Mere, Sharan Gahoon Kiski ।
Tum Bin Aur Na Dooja, Aas Karoon Jiski ॥
Om Jai Jagdish Hare

Tum Pooran Parmatma, Tum Antaryami ।
Paar Brahma Parmeshwar, Tum Sabke Swami ॥
Om Jai Jagdish Hare

Tum Karuna Ke Saagar, Tum Palankarta ।
Main Moorakh Kaal Kaami, Kripa Karo Bharta ॥
Om Jai Jagdish Hare

Tum Ho Ek Agauchar, Sabke Praanpati ।
Kis Vidhi Miloon Dayamay, Tumko Main Kumati ॥
Om Jai Jagdish Hare

Deenbandhu, Dukhharata Tum Thakur Mere ।
Apne Haath Uthao, Dwaar Pade Tere ॥
Om Jai Jagdish Hare

Vishay Vikaar Mitaao, Paap Haro Deva ।
Shraddha-Bhakti Badaao, Santan Ki Seva ॥
Om Jai Jagdish Hare

श्री मायातीत विष्णु जी की आरती

जय जगदीश हरे, प्रभु! जय जगदीश हरे।
मायातीत, महेश्वर मन-वच-बुद्धि परे॥
जय जगदीश हरे

आदि, अनादि, अगोचर, अविचल, अविनाशी।
अतुल, अनन्त, अनामय, अमित, शक्ति-राशि॥
जय जगदीश हरे

अमल, अकल, अज, अक्षय, अव्यय, अविकारी।
सत-चित-सुखमय, सुन्दर शिव सत्ताधारी॥
जय जगदीश हरे

विधि-हरि-शंकर-गणपति-सूर्य-शक्तिरूपा।
विश्व चराचर तुम ही, तुम ही विश्वभूपा॥
जय जगदीश हरे

माता-पिता-पितामह-स्वामि-सुहृद्-भर्ता।
विश्वोत्पादक पालक रक्षक संहर्ता॥
जय जगदीश हरे

साक्षी, शरण, सखा, प्रिय प्रियतम, पूर्ण प्रभो।
केवल-काल कलानिधि, कालातीत, विभो ।।
जय जगदीश हरे

राम-कृष्ण करुणामय, प्रेमामृत-सागर।
मन-मोहन मुरलीधर नित-नव नटनागर ।।
जय जगदीश हरे

सब विधि-हीन, मलिन-मति, हम अति पातकि-जन।
प्रभुपद-विमुख अभागी, कलि-कलुषित तन मन ।।
जय जगदीश हरे

आश्रय-दान दयार्णव! हम सबको दीजै।
पाप-ताप हर हरि! सब, निज-जन कर लीजै ।।
जय जगदीश हर

Shri Mayateet Vishnu Ji Ki Aarti

Jai Jagdish Hare, Prabhu! Jai Jagdish Hare
Mayateet, Maheshwar Man-Vach-Buddhi Pare ||
Jai Jagdish Hare

Aadi, Anadi, Agauchar, Avichal, Avinaashi
Atul, Anant, Anamay, Amit, Shakti-Rashi ||
Jai Jagdish Hare

Amal, Akal, Aj, Akshaya, Avyaya, Avikari
Sat-Chit-Sukhmay, Sundar Shiv Sattadhari ||
Jai Jagdish Hare

Vidhi-Hari-Shankar-Ganapati-Surya-Shaktiroopa
Vishw Charachar Tum Hi, Tum Hi Vishwabhupa ||
Jai Jagdish Hare

Mata-Pita-Pitamaha-Swami-Suhrit-Bharta
Vishwotpadi Palak Rakshak Sanhartaa ||
Jai Jagdish Hare

Saakshi, Sharan, Sakha, Priya Priyatam, Poorn Prabho
Keval-Kaal Kalanidhi, Kaalateet, Vibho ॥
Jai Jagdish Hare

Ram-Krishna Karunamay, Premamrit-Saagar
Man-Mohan Muraliadhar Nit-Nav Natanagar ॥
Jai Jagdish Hare

Sab Vidhi-Hin, Malin-Mati, Ham Ati Paathaki-Jan
Prabhu-Pad-Vimukh Abhaagi, Kali-Kalushit Tan Man ॥
Jai Jagdish Hare

Aashray-Daan Dayarnav! Ham Sabko Deeje
Paap-Tap Har Hari! Sab, Nija-Jan Kar Leejay ॥
Jai Jagdish Hare

श्री सत्यानारायण जी की आरती

ॐ जय लक्ष्मीरमणा स्वामी जय लक्ष्मीरमणा।
सत्यनारायण स्वामी, जन पातक हरणा
ॐ जय लक्ष्मीरमणा स्वामी....

रत्नजडित सिंहासन, अद्भुत छवि राजे।
नारद करत निरतंर घंटा ध्वनी बाजे।।
ॐ जय लक्ष्मीरमणा स्वामी....

प्रकट भयें कलिकारण, द्विज को दरस दियो।
बूढों ब्राम्हण बनके, कंचन महल कियो।।
ॐ जय लक्ष्मीरमणा स्वामी.....

दुर्बल भील कठार, जिन पर कृपा करी।
चंद्रचूड एक राजा तिनकी विपत्ति हरी।।
ॐ जय लक्ष्मीरमणा स्वामी.....

वैश्य मनोरथ पायो, श्रद्धा तज दीन्ही।
सो फल भोग्यो प्रभुजी, फिर स्तुति किन्ही।।
ॐ जय लक्ष्मीरमणा स्वामी.....

भाव भक्ति के कारण छिन छिन रूप धर्यो।
श्रद्धा धारण कीन्ही, तिनके काज सरें ।।
ॐ जय लक्ष्मीरमणा स्वामी.....

ग्वाल बाल संग राजा, वन में भक्ति करी।
मनवांछित फल दीन्ह्यो, दीन दयालु हरि ।।
ॐ जय लक्ष्मीरमणा स्वामी.....

चढत प्रसाद सवायों, कदली फल मेवा।
धूप दीप तुलसी से राजी सत्य देवा ।।
ॐ जय लक्ष्मीरमणा स्वामी.....

सत्यनारायणजी की आरती जो कोई नर गावे।
ऋद्धि सिद्धि सुख संपत्ति सहज रूप पावे ।।
ॐ जय लक्ष्मीरमणा स्वामी.....
ॐ जय लक्ष्मीरमणा स्वामी जय लक्ष्मीरमणा।
सत्यनारायण स्वामी, जन पातक हरणा ।।

Shri Satyanarayan Ji Ki Aarti

Om Jai Lakshmeeramana Swami Jai Lakshmeeramana
Satyanarayan Swami, Jan Paathak Harana
Om Jai Lakshmeeramana Swami....

Ratn-Jadit Singh-San, Adbhut Chavi Raajay
Narad Karat Nirantar Ghanta Dhvani Baajay ||
Om Jai Lakshmeeramana Swami....

Prakat Bhayen Kalikaaran, Dwij Ko Darshan Diya
Boodhon Brahman Banke, Kanchan Mahal Kiyon ||
Om Jai Lakshmeeramana Swami.....

Durbal Bheel Kathar, Jin Par Kripa Kari
Chandachud Ek Raja Tinki Vipatti Hari ||
Om Jai Lakshmeeramana Swami.....

Vaishya Manorath Paayo, Shraddha Taj Dinhi
So Phal Bhogyo Prabhuji, Pher Stuti Kihi ||
Om Jai Lakshmeeramana Swami.....

Bhav Bhakti Ke Karan, Chhin Chhin Rup Dharen
Shraddha Dharan Kihi, Tinke Kaaj Saren II
Om Jai Lakshmeeramana Swami.....

Gwal-Baal Sang Raja, Van Mein Bhakti Kari
Manvanchit Phal Dinho, Deen Dayalu Hari II
Om Jai Lakshmeeramana Swami.....

Chadhat Prasad savayo, Kadali Phal Meva
Dhoop Deep Tulsi Se Raaji Satya Deva II
Om Jai Lakshmeeramana Swami.....

Satyanarayan Ji Ki Aarti Jo Koi Nar Gaave
Riddhi Siddhi Sukh Sampatti Sahaj Rup Paave II
Om Jai Lakshmeeramana Swami.....
Om Jai Lakshmeeramana Swami Jai Lakshmeeramana
Satyanarayan Swami, Jan Paathak Harana

श्री रामचन्द्र जी की आरती

श्री रामचन्द्र कृपालु भजु मन हरण भवभय दारुणं।
नवकंज लोचन, कंजमुख, करकंज, पदकंजारुणं॥

श्री रामचन्द्र कृपालु भजु मन हरण भवभय दारुणं।
श्री राम श्री राम....
कंदर्प अगणित अमित छबि, नवनीलनीरद सुन्दरं।
पट पीत मानहु तड़ित रुचि शुचि नौमि जनक सुतावरं॥

श्री रामचन्द्र कृपालु भजु मन हरण भवभय दारुणं।
श्री राम श्री राम....
भजु दीनबंधु दिनेश दानव दैत्यवंशनिकंदनं।
रघुनंद आंनदकंद कौसलचंद दशरथनंदनं॥

श्री रामचन्द्र कृपालु भजु मन हरण भवभय दारुणं।
श्री राम श्री राम...
सिर मुकुट कुंडल तिलक चारु उदारु अंग विभूषणं।
आजानु भुजा शर चाप धर, संग्राम जित खर दूषणं॥

श्री रामचन्द्र कृपालु भजु मन हरण भवभय दारुणं

इति वदित तुलसीदास शंकरशेषमुनिमनरंजनं।

मम ह्रदयकंजनिवास कुरु, कमदि खल दल गंजनं॥

श्री रामचन्द्र कृपालु भजु मन हरण भवभय दारुणं।

नवकंज लोचन, कंजमुख, करकुंज, पदकंजारुणं॥

श्री राम श्री राम..

Shri Ramchandra Ji Ki Aarti

Shri Ramchandra Kripalu Bhaj Man, Haran Bhavbhay Daarun

Navkanj Lochan, Kanjmukh, Karkunj, Padkanjarun

Shri Ramchandra Kripalu Bhaj Man, Haran Bhavbhay Daarun

Shri Ram Shri Ram....

Kandarpa Aganit Amit Chhavi, Navneelneerad Sundaram

Pat Peet Maanhu Tadit Ruchi Shuchi Naumi Janak Sutavaram

Shri Ramchandra Kripalu Bhaj Man, Haran Bhavbhay Daarun

Shri Ram Shri Ram....

Bhaju Deenbandhu Dinesh Danav Daityavansh nikanandanam

Raghunand Anandkand Kausalchand Dashrathnandan

Shri Ramchandra Kripalu Bhaj Man, Haran Bhavbhay Daarun

Shri Ram Shri Ram...

Sir Mukut Kundal Tilak Charu Udaru Ang Vibhushan

Ajanubhuja Shara Chaap Dhara, Sangram Jit Khar Dushan

Shri Ramchandra Kripalu Bhaj Man, Haran Bhavbhay Daarun

Iti Vadhit Tulsidas Shankarsheeshmuni Manranjan

Mam Hridaykanjanivaas Kuru, Kamadi Khaal Dal Ganjanam

Shri Ramchandra Kripalu Bhaj Man, Haran Bhavbhay Daarun

Navkanj Lochan, Kanjmukh, Karkunj, Padkanjarun

Shri Ram Shri Ram...

श्री हनुमान जी की आरती

आरती कीजे हनुमान लला की ।
दुष्ट दलन रघुनाथ कला की ।।
जाके बल से गिरवर कांपे ।
रोग दोष जाके निकट ना झांके ।।
अंजनी पुत्र महा बलदाई ।
संतन के प्रभु सदा सहाई ।।
दे वीरा रघुनाथ पठाये ।
लंका जारि सिया सुधी लाये ।।
लंका सी कोट संमदर सी खाई ।
जात पवनसुत बार न लाई ।।
लंका जारि असुर संहारे ।
सियाराम जी के काज संवारे ।।
लक्ष्मण मुर्छित पड़े सकारे ।
आनि संजीवन प्राण उबारे ।।
पैठि पताल तोरि जम कारे ।
अहिरावन की भुजा उखारे ।।
बायें भुजा असुर दल मारे ।
दाहिने भुजा संतजन तारे ।।

सुर नर मुनि जन आरती उतारे ।
जै जै जै हनुमान उचारे ।।
कचंन थाल कपूर लौ छाई ।
आरती करत अंजना माई ।।
जो हनुमान जी की आरती गाये ।
बसि बैकुंठ परम पद पाये ।।
लंका विध्वंस किये रघुराई ।
तुलसीदास स्वामी कीर्ति गाई ।।
आरती कीजे हनुमान लला की ।
दुष्ट दलन रघुनाथ कला की

Shri Hanuman Ji Ki Aarti

Aarti Kije Hanuman Lala Ki
Dusht Dalan Raghunath Kala Ki
Jake Bal Se Girvar Kaampe
Rog Dosh Jake Nikat Na Jhaanke
Anjani Putra Maha Baldaai
Santaan Ke Prabhu Sadaa Sahaai
De Veera Raghunath Pathaaye
Lanka Jaari Siya Sudhi Laaye
Lanka Se Koti Samundar Se Khaayi
Jaat Pavan Sut Baar Na Laayi
Lanka Jaari Asur Sanghaare
Siyaram Ji Ke Kaaj Sanwaare
Lakshman Murchhit Padhe Sakare
Aani Sanjeevan Praan Ubaare
Paithi Patal Tor Jam Kaare
Ahiravan Ki Bhujha Ukhaare
Baaye Bhujha Asur Dal Maare
Daheene Bhujha Sab Sant Jan Taare

Sur Nar Muni Jan Aarti Utaare
Jai Jai Jai Hanuman Uchhaare
Kanchan Thaal Kapoor Lau Chhaayi
Aarti Karat Anjana Maayi
Jo Hanuman Ji Ki Aarti Gaye
Basin Vaikunth Param Pad Paaye
Lanka Vidhwams Kiye Raghurayi
Tulsidas Swami Kirti Gayi
Aarti Kije Hanuman Lala Ki
Dusht Dalan Raghunath Kala Ki

श्री शिव जी की आरती

जय शिव ओंकारा हर ॐ शिव ओंकारा।
ब्रम्हा विष्णु सदाशिव अर्द्धांगी धारा।।
ॐ जय शिव ओंकारा......

एकानन चतुरानन पंचांनन राजे।
हंसासंन, गरुड़ासन, वृषवाहन साजे।।
ॐ जय शिव ओंकारा......

दो भुज चारु चतुर्भज दस भुज अति सोहें।
तीनों रुप निरखता त्रिभुवन जन मोहें।।
ॐ जय शिव ओंकारा......

अक्षमाला, बनमाला, रुण्डमालाधारी।
चंदन, मृगमद सोहें, भाले शशिधारी।।
ॐ जय शिव ओंकारा......

श्वेताम्बर, पीताम्बर, बाघाम्बर अंगे
सनकादिक, ब्रम्हादिक, भूतादिक संगे
ॐ जय शिव ओंकारा......

कर के मध्य कमंडलु चक्र, त्रिशूल धरता।
जगकर्ता, जगभर्ता, जगसंहारकर्ता ।।
ॐ जय शिव ओंकारा......

ब्रम्हा विष्णु सदाशिव जानत अविवेका।
प्रणवाक्षर मध्ये ये तीनों एका ।।
ॐ जय शिव ओंकारा......

काशी में विश्वनाथ विराजत नन्दी ब्रम्हचारी।
नित उठि भोग लगावत महिमा अति भारी ।।
ॐ जय शिव ओंकारा......

त्रिगुण शिवजी की आरती जो कोई नर गावे ।
कहत शिवानंद स्वामी मनवांछित फल पावे ।।
ॐ जय शिव ओंकारा.....

जय शिव ओंकारा हर ॐ शिव ओंकारा।
ब्रम्हा विष्णु सदाशिव अर्द्धांगी धारा ।।
ॐ जय शिव ओंकारा.....

Shri Shiv Ji Ki Aarti

Jai Shiv Omkara, Har Om Shiv Omkara
Brahma Vishnu Sadaashiva Arddhaangi Dhaara
Om Jai Shiv Omkara...

Ekaanana Chaturanana Panchaanana Raaje
Hamsaasana, Garudaasana, Vrishavaahana Saaje
Om Jai Shiv Omkara...

Do Bhuj Chaaru Chaturbhuj Das Bhuj Ati Sohe
Teeno Roop Nirkhta Tribhuvan Jan Mohe
Om Jai Shiv Omkara...

Akshamaala, Banmaala, Rundamaalaadhari
Chandan, Mrigamada Sohe, Bhaale Shashidhari
Om Jai Shiv Omkara...

Shvetambhar, Peetambhar, Baaghambar Ange
Sanakadik, Brahmadik, Bhootadik Sange
Om Jai Shiv Omkara...

Kar Ke Madhya Kamandal, Chakra, Trishool Dharata
Jagkartaa, Jagbharta, Jagsanhaarkarta
Om Jai Shiv Omkara...

Brahma Vishnu Sadaashiva Jaanat Aviveka
Pravankshar Madhye Ye Teenon Eka
Om Jai Shiv Omkara...

Kashi Mein Vishwanath Virajat Nandi Brahmachari
Nit Uthi Bhog Lagavat Mahima Ati Bhaari
Om Jai Shiv Omkara...

Trigun Shivji Ki Aarti Jo Koi Nar Gaave
Kahat Shivaanand Swami Manvanchhit Phal Paave
Om Jai Shiv Omkara...

Jai Shiv Omkara, Har Om Shiv Omkara
Brahma Vishnu Sadaashiva Addhaangi Dhaara
Om Jai Shiv Omkara...

श्री कृष्ण जी की आरती

ॐ जय श्री कृष्ण हरे, प्रभु जय श्री कृष्ण हरे
भक्तन के दुख टारे पल में दूर करे.
जय जय श्री कृष्ण हरे....

परमानन्द मुरारी मोहन गिरधारी.
जय रस रास बिहारी जय जय गिरधारी.
जय जय श्री कृष्ण हरे....

कर कंचन कटि कंचन श्रुति कुण्डल माला
मोर मुकुट पीताम्बर सोहे बनमाला.
जय जय श्री कृष्ण हरे....

दीन सुदामा तारे, दरिद्र दुख टारे.
जग के फंद छुड़ाए, भव सागर तारे.
जय जय श्री कृष्ण हरे....

हिरण्यकश्यप संहारे नरहरि रुप धरे.
पाहन से प्रभु प्रगटे जन के बीच पड़े.
जय जय श्री कृष्ण हरे....

केशी कंस विदारे नर कुबेर तारे.
दामोदर छवि सुन्दर भगतन रखवारे.
जय जय श्री कृष्ण हरे....

काली नाग नथैया नटवर छवि सोहे.
फन फन चढ़त ही नागन, नागन मन मोहे.
जय जय श्री कृष्ण हरे....

राज्य विभिषण थापे सीता शोक हरे.
द्रुपद सुता पत राखी करुणा लाज भरे.
जय जय श्री कृष्ण हरे....
ॐ जय श्री कृष्ण हरे

Shri Krishna Ji Ki Aarti

Om Jai Shri Krishna Hare, Prabhu Jai Shri Krishna Hare
Bhaktan Ke Dukh Tare Pal Mein Door Kare
Jai Jai Shri Krishna Hare...

Parmanand Murari Mohan Girdhari
Jai Ras Raas Bihari Jai Jai Girdhari
Jai Jai Shri Krishna Hare...

Kar Kanchan Kati Kanchan Shruti Kundal Maala
Mor Mukut Peetambar Sohe Banmaala
Jai Jai Shri Krishna Hare...

Deen Sudama Taare, Daridra Dukh Taare
Jag Ke Phand Chhudaaye, Bhav Saagar Taare
Jai Jai Shri Krishna Hare...

Hiranyakashyap Sanhaare Narhari Roop Dhare
Pahan Se Prabhu Pragate Jan Ke Beech Pade
Jai Jai Shri Krishna Hare...

Keshi Kansa Vidhaare Nar Kuber Taare
Damodar Chhavi Sundar Bhaktan Rakhwaare
Jai Jai Shri Krishna Hare...

Kaali Naag Nathaiya Natvar Chhavi Sohe
Fan Fan Chadhat Hi Naagan, Naagan Man Mohe
Jai Jai Shri Krishna Hare...

Rajya Vibhishan Thaape Sita Shok Hare
Drupad Suta Pat Raakhi Karuna Laaj Bhare
Jai Jai Shri Krishna Hare...
Om Jai Shri Krishna Hare

श्री कुंज बिहारी की आरती

आरती कुंजबिहारी की, श्री गिरिधर कृष्णमुरारी की ॥
गले में बैजंती माला, बजावै मुरली मधुर बाला।
श्रवण में कुण्डल झलकाला, नंद के आनंद नंदलाला।
गगन सम अंग कांति काली, राधिका चमक रही आली।
लतन में ठाढ़े बनमाली; भ्रमर सी अलक, कस्तूरी तिलक,
चंद्र सी झलक; ललित छवि श्यामा प्यारी की ॥
श्री गिरिधर कृष्णमुरारी की...
कनकमय मोर मुकुट बिलसै, देवता दरसन को तरसैं।
गगन सों सुमन रासि बरसै; बजे मुरचंग, मधुर मिरदंग,
ग्वालिन संग; अतुल रति गोप कुमारी की ॥
श्री गिरिधर कृष्णमुरारी की...
जहां ते प्रकट भई गंगा, कलुष कलि हारिणि श्रीगंगा।
स्मरन ते होत मोह भंगा; बसी सिव सीस, जटा के बीच,
हरै अघ कीच; चरन छवि श्रीबनवारी की ॥
श्री गिरिधर कृष्णमुरारी की...
चमकती उज्ज्वल तट रेनू, बज रही वृंदावन बेनू।
चहुं दिसि गोपि ग्वाल धेनू; हंसत मृदु मंद, चांदनी चंद,
कटत भव फंद; टेर सुन दीन भिखारी की ॥
श्री गिरिधर कृष्णमुरारी की...

Shri Kunj Bihari Ki Aarti

Aarti Kunjbihari Ki, Shri Giridhar Krishnamurari Ki

Gale Mein Baijanti Maala, Bajave Muralimadhur Baala

Shravan Mein Kundal Jhalkaala, Nand Ke Anand Nandala

Gagan Sam Ang Kaanti Kaali, Radhika Chamak Rahi Aali

Latan Mein Thaade Banmaali, Bhramar Si Alak, Kasturi Tilak

Chandra Si Jhalak, Lalit Chhavi Shyaama Pyari Ki

Shri Giridhar Krishnamurari Ki...

Kanakmay Mor Mukut Bilasai, Devata Darshan Ko Tarasai

Gagan Son Suman Raasi Barsai, Baje Murchang, Madhur Miradang

Gwaalin Sang, Atul Rati Gop Kumari Ki

Shri Giridhar Krishnamurari Ki...

Jahan Te Prakat Bhai Ganga, Kalush Kali Haari Shri Ganga

Smaran Te Hot Moh Bhanga, Basi Shiv Sees, Jata Ke Beech

Harai Agh Keech, Charan Chhavi Shrivanwaari Ki

Shri Giridhar Krishnamurari Ki...

Chamakti Ujjwal Tat Renu, Baj Rahi Vrindavan Benu

Chahun Disi Gopi Gwaal Dhenoo, Hansat Mridu Mand, Chandni Chand

Katat Bhav Phand, Ter Sun Deen Bhikhari Ki

Shri Giridhar Krishnamurari Ki

श्री चित्रगुप्त जी की आरती

ॐ जय चित्रगुप्त हरे, स्वामी जय चित्रगुप्त हरे।
भक्त जनों के इच्छित, फल को पूर्ण करे॥
ॐ जय चित्रगुप्त हरे... ॥

विघ्न विनाशक मंगलकर्ता, सन्तन सुखदायी।
भक्तन के प्रतिपालक, त्रिभुवन यश छायी॥
ॐ जय चित्रगुप्त हरे... ॥

रूप चतुर्भुज, श्यामल मूरति, पीताम्बर राजै।
मातु इरावती, दक्षिणा, वाम अङ्ग साजै॥
ॐ जय चित्रगुप्त हरे... ॥

कष्ट निवारण, दुष्ट संहारण, प्रभु अन्तर्यामी।
सृष्टि संहारण, जन दुःख हारण, प्रकट हुये स्वामी॥
ॐ जय चित्रगुप्त हरे... ॥

कलम, दवात, शङ्ख, पत्रिका, कर में अति सोहै।
वैजयन्ती वनमाला, त्रिभुवन मन मोहै॥
ॐ जय चित्रगुप्त हरे... ॥

सिंहासन का कार्य सम्भाला, ब्रह्मा हर्षाये।
तैंतीस कोटि देवता, चरणन में धाये॥
ॐ जय चित्रगुप्त हरे... ॥

नृपति सौदास, भीष्म पितामह, याद तुम्हें कीन्हा।
वेगि विलम्ब न लायो, इच्छित फल दीन्हा॥
ॐ जय चित्रगुप्त हरे... ॥

दारा, सुत, भगिनी, सब अपने स्वास्थ के कर्ता।
जाऊं कहां शरण में किसकी, तुम तज मैं भर्ता॥
ॐ जय चित्रगुप्त हरे... ॥

बन्धु, पिता तुम स्वामी, शरण गहूं किसकी।
तुम बिन और न दूजा, आस करूँ जिसकी॥
ॐ जय चित्रगुप्त हरे... ॥

जो जन चित्रगुप्त जी की आरती, प्रेम सहित गावैं।
चौरासी से निश्चित छूटैं, इच्छित फल पावैं॥
ॐ जय चित्रगुप्त हरे... ॥

न्यायाधीश बैकुण्ठ निवासी, पाप पुण्य लिखते।
हम हैं शरण तिहारी, आस न दूजी करते॥
ॐ जय चित्रगुप्त हरे... ॥

Shri Chitragupt Ji Ki Aarti

Om Jai Chitragupt Hare, Swami Jai Chitragupt Hare
Bhakta Jano Ke Ichhit, Phal Ko Poorn Kare
Om Jai Chitragupt Hare...

Vighna Vinashak Mangalkarta, Santan Sukhdaayi
Bhaktan Ke Pratipaalak, Tribhuvan Yash Chhaayi
Om Jai Chitragupt Hare...

Roop Chaturbhuj, Shyaamala Moorti, Peetambar Raajai
Maatu Iravati, Dakshina, Vaam Ang Saajai
Om Jai Chitragupt Hare...

Kasht Nivaran, Dusht Sanhaar, Prabhu Antaryami
Srishti Sanhaar, Jan Dukh Haaran, Prakat Hue Swami
Om Jai Chitragupt Hare...

Kalam, Davaat, Shankh, Patrika, Kar Mein Ati Sohei
Vaijayanti Vanmaala, Tribhuvan Man Mohai
Om Jai Chitragupt Hare...

Singhasan Ka Kaary Sambhaala, Brahma Harshaaye
Taintee Koty Devata, Charanon Mein Dhaaye
Om Jai Chitragupt Hare...

Nripati Saudasa, Bhishma Pitamah, Yaad Tumhe Keenha
Vegi Vilamb Na Laayo, Ichhit Phal Deenha
Om Jai Chitragupt Hare...

Daara, Sut, Bhagini, Sab Apne Svasth Ke Karta
Jaaoon Kahan Sharan Mein Kiski, Tum Taj Main Bharta
Om Jai Chitragupt Hare...

Bandhu, Pita Tum Swami, Sharan Gaho Kiski
Tum Bin Aur Na Dooja, Aas Karoon Jiski
Om Jai Chitragupt Hare...

Jo Jan Chitragupt Ji Ki Aarti, Prem Sahit Gaave
Chaurasi Se Nischit Chhootain, Ichhit Phal Paave
Om Jai Chitragupt Hare...

Nyayadhish Baikunth Nivasi, Paap Punya Likhte
Hum Hain Sharan Tihari, Aas Na Dooji Karte
Om Jai Chitragupt Hare...

श्री शनि देव जी की आरती

जय जय श्री शनिदेव भक्तन हितकारी।
सूरज के पुत्र प्रभु छाया महतारी॥ जय॥

श्याम अंक वक्र दृष्ट चतुर्भुजा धारी।
नीलाम्बर धार नाथ गज की असवारी॥ जय... ॥

किरीट मुकुट शीश रजित दीपत है लिलारी।
मुक्तन की माला गले शोभित बलिहारी॥ जय... ॥

मोदक मिष्ठान पान चढ़त हैं सुपारी।
लोहा तिल तेल उड़द महिषी अति प्यारी॥ जय... ॥

देव दनुज ऋषि मुनि सुमरिन नर नारी।
विश्वनाथ धरत ध्यान शरण हैं तुम्हारी॥ जय... ॥

Shri Shani Dev Ji Ki Aarti

Jai Jai Shri Shani Dev Bhaktan Hitkaari
Suraj Ke Putra Prabhu Chhaya Mahataari ॥ Jai... ॥

Shyaam Ank Wakar Drishti Chaturbhuj Dhaari
Neelambar Dhar Naath Gaj Ki Aswaari ॥ Jai... ॥

Kireet Mukut Sheesh Rajit Deepat Hai Lilari
Muktan Ki Maala Gale Shobhit Balihari ॥ Jai... ॥

Modak Mishtaan Paan Chhat Hai Supaari
Loha Til Tel Urd Mahishi Ati Pyari ॥ Jai... ॥

Dev Danuj Rishi Muni Smaran Nar Naari
Vishwanath Dharat Dhyaan Sharan Hai Tumhaari ॥ Jai... ॥

श्री बृहस्पति देव की आरती

जय बृहस्पति देवा, ऊँ जय बृहस्पति देवा।
छि छिन भोग लगाऊं, कदली फल मेवा ।।

तुम पूरण परमात्मा, तुम अन्तर्यामी।
जगतपिता जगदीश्वर, तुम सबके स्वामी ।।

चरणामृत निज निर्मल, सब पातक हर्ता।
सकल मनोरथ दायक, कृपा करो भर्ता ।।

तन, मन, धन अर्पण कर, जो जन शरण पड़े।
प्रभु प्रकट तब होकर, आकर द्वार खड़े ।।

दीनदयाल दयानिधि, भक्तन हितकारी।
पाप दोष सब हर्ता, भव बंधन हारी ।।

सकल मनोरथ दायक, सब संशय तारो।
विषय विकार मिटाओ, संतन सुखकारी ।।

जो कोई आरती तेरी, प्रेम सहत गावे।
जेठानन्द आनन्दकर, सो निश्चय पावे ।।

Shri Brihaspati Dev Ki Aarti

Jai Brihaspati Deva, Om Jai Brihaspati Deva
Chhi Chhin Bhog Lagao, Kadali Phal Meva

Tum Puran Parmatma, Tum Antaryami
Jagatpita Jagadishwar, Tum Sabke Swami

Charan Amrit Niji Nirmal, Sab Paathak Harta
Sakal Manorath Daayak, Kripa Karo Bharta

Tan, Man, Dhan Arpan Kar, Jo Jan Sharan Pade
Prabhu Prakat Tab Hokar, Aakar Dwaar Khade

Deendayal Dayanidhi, Bhaktan Hitkaari
Paap Dosh Sab Harta, Bhav Bandhan Haari

Sakal Manorath Daayak, Sab Sanshay Taaro
Vishay Vikaar Mitao, Santan Sukhkaari

Jo Koi Aarti Teri, Prem Sahit Gaave
Jethanand Anandkar, So Nishchay Paave

श्री सूर्य देव की आरती

ऊँ जय सूर्य भगवान, जय हो दिनकर भगवान।
जगत् के नेत्र स्वरूपा, तुम हो त्रिगुण स्वरूपा।
धरत सब ही तव ध्यान, ऊँ जय सूर्य भगवान।।
सारथी अरुण हैं प्रभु तुम, श्वेत कमलधारी।
तुम चार भुजाधारी।।
अश्व हैं सात तुम्हारे, कोटि किरण पसारे। तुम हो देव महान।।
ऊँ जय सूर्य ...
ऊषाकाल में जब तुम, उदयाचल आते। सब तब दर्शन पाते।।
फैलाते उजियारा जागता तब जग सारा। करे सब तब गुणगान।।
ऊँ जय सूर्य ...
संध्या में भुवनेश्वर अस्ताचल जाते। गोधन तब घर आते।।
गोधुली बेला में हर घर हर आंगन में। हो तव महिमा गान।।
ऊँ जय सूर्य ...
देव दनुज नर नारी ऋषी-मुनी वर भजते। आदित्य हृदय जपते।।
स्त्रोत ये मंगलकारी, इसकी है रचना न्यारी। दे नव जीवनदान।।
ऊँ जय सूर्य ...
तुम हो त्रिकाल रचियता, तुम जग के आधार। महिमा तब अपरम्पार।।
प्राणों का सिंचन करके भक्तों को अपने देते। बल बृद्धि और

ज्ञान ।। ऊँ जय सूर्य ...

भूचर जल चर खेचर, सब के हो प्राण तुम्हीं। सब जीवों के प्राण तुम्हीं ।।

वेद पुराण बखाने धर्म सभी तुम्हें माने। तुम ही सर्व शक्तिमान ।। ऊँ जय सूर्य ...

पूजन करती दिशाएं पूजे दश दिक्पाल। तुम भुवनों के प्रतिपाल ।।

ऋतुएं तुम्हारी दासी, तुम शाश्वत अविनाशी।

शुभकारी अंशमान ।। ऊँ जय सूर्य ...

ऊँ जय सूर्य भगवान, जय हो दिनकर भगवान।

जगत के नेत्र रूवरूपा, तुम हो त्रिगुण स्वरूपा ।।

धरत सब ही तव ध्यान, ऊँ जय सूर्य भगवान ।।

Shri Surya Dev Ki Aarti

Om Jai Surya Bhagwan, Jai Ho Dinkar Bhagwan
Jagat Ke Netra Svarupa, Tum Ho Trigun Svarupa
Dhara Sabhi Tava Dhyaan, Om Jai Surya Bhagwan
Saarthi Arun Hai Prabhu Tum, Shvet Kamaladhari
Tum Chaar
Bhujadhari
Ashw Hai Saat Tumhare, Koti Kiran Pasare
Tum Ho Dev Mahaaan
Om Jai Surya...
Ushakal Mein Jab Tum, Udayachal Aate
Sab Tab Darshan Paate
Phailate Ujjiyara Jaagta Tab Jag Saara
Kare Sab Tab Gungaan
Om Jai Surya...
Sandhya Mein Bhuwanshwar Astachal Jaate
Godhan Tab Ghar Aate
Godhuli Bela Mein Har Ghar Har Aangan Mein
Ho Tava Mahima Gaan
Om Jai Surya...
Dev Danuj Nar Naari Rishi Muni Var Bhajate

Aditya Hriday Jpate

Stotra Ye Mangalkari, Iski Hai Rachna Nyari

De Nav Jeevandaan

Om Jai Surya…

Tum ho trikaal rachiyata, tum jag ke aadhar. Mahima tab aparampaar.

Pranon ka sinchan karke bhakton ko apne dete. Bal vruddhi aur gyaan.

Om jaya surya...

Bhoochar jalchar khechar, sab ke ho praan tumhi. Sab jeevon ke praan tumhi.

Veda puraan bakhaane dharm sabhi tumhe maane. Tum hi sarv shaktimaan.

Om jaya surya...

Poojan karti dishaayein pooje dash dikpaal. Tum bhuvon ke pratipaal.

Rituein tumhaari daasi, tum shaasvat avinaashi. Shubhkaari anshamaan.

Om jaya surya...

Om jaya surya bhagwaan, jaya ho dinakar bhagwaan.

Jagat ke netra ruvaroopa, tum ho trigun svaroopa.

Dharti sabhi tava dhyaan, Om jaya surya bhagwaan.

श्री दुर्गा जी की आरती

जय अम्बे गौरी, मैया जय श्यामा गौरी
तुम को निस दिन ध्यावत
मैयाजी को निस दिन ध्यावत हरि ब्रह्मा शिवजी ।। जय अम्बे गौरी ।।

माँग सिन्दूर विराजत टीको मृग मद को। मैया टीको मृगमद को
उज्ज्वल से दो नैना चन्द्रवदन नीको ।। जय अम्बे गौरी ।।

कनक समान कलेवर रक्ताम्बर साजे। मैया रक्ताम्बर साजे
रक्त पुष्प गले माला कण्ठन पर साजे ।। जय अम्बे गौरी ।।

केहरि वाहन राजत खड्ग खप्परधारी। मैया खड्ग खप्परधारी
सुर नर मुनि जन सेवत तिनके दुख हारी ।। जय अम्बे गौरी ।।

कानन कुण्डल शोभित नासाग्रे मोती। मैया नासाग्रे मोती
कोटिक चन्द्र दिवाकर सम राजत ज्योति ।। जय अम्बे गौरी ।।

शुम्भ निशुंभ बिदारे महिषासुर घाती। मैया महिषासुर घाती
धूम्र विलोचन नैना निशदिन मदमाती।। जय अम्बे गौरी ।।

चण्ड मुण्ड संहारे शोणित बीज हरे। मैया शोणित बीज हरे
मधु कैटभ दोउ मारे सुर भयहीन करे।। जय अम्बे गौरी।।

ब्रह्माणी रुद्राणी तुम कमला रानी। मैया तुम कमला रानी
आगम निगम बखानी तुम शिव पटरानी।। जय अम्बे गौरी।।

चौंसठ योगिन गावत नृत्य करत भैरों। मैया नृत्य करत भैरों
बाजत ताल मृदंगा और बाजत डमरू।। जय अम्बे गौरी।।

तुम हो जग की माता तुम ही हो भर्ता। मैया तुम ही हो भर्ता
भक्तन की दुख हर्ता सुख सम्पति कर्ता।। जय अम्बे गौरी।।

भुजा चार अति शोभित वर मुद्रा धारी। मैया वर मुद्रा धारी
मन वाँछित फल पावत देवता नर नारी।। जय अम्बे गौरी।।

कंचन थाल विराजत अगर कपूर बाती। मैया अगर कपूर बाती
श्रीमालकेतु में राजत कोटि रतन ज्योती।। बोलो जय अम्बे गौरी।।

माँ अम्बे की आरती जो कोई नर गावे। मैया जो कोई नर गावे
कहत शिवानन्द स्वामी सुख सम्पति पावे।। जय अम्बे गौरी।।

देवी वन्दना

या देवी सर्वभूतेषु शक्तिरूपेण संस्थिता।
नमस्तस्यै नमस्तस्यै नमस्तस्यै नमो नमः ॥

Shri Durga Ji Ki Aarti

Jai Ambe Gauri, Maiya Jai Shyama Gauri
Tum ko nis din dhyavat
Maiyaji ko nis din dhyavat Hari Brahma Shivji.
Jai Ambe Gauri.

Maang Sindoor Virajat Tiko Mrig Mad Ko.
Maiya Tiko Mrigmad Ko
Ujjwal se do Naina Chandravadana Neeko.
Jai Ambe Gauri.

Kanak Sama Kelevar Raktambar Saaje.
Maiya Raktambar Saaje
Rakt Pushp Gale Mala kanthan per Saaje.
Jai Ambe Gauri.

Keheri Vahan Rajat Khadg Kripan Dhaari.
Maiya Khadg Kripan Dhaari
Sur Nar Muni Jan Sevat Tinke Dukh Haari.
Jai Ambe Gauri.

Kanan Kundal Shobhit Nasagre Moti.
Maiya Nasagre Moti
Kotik Chandra Divakar Sam Rajat Jyoti.
Jai Ambe Gauri.

Shumbh Nishambhu Vidare Mahishasur Ghati.
Maiya Mahishasur Ghati
Dhoomra Vilochan Naina Nishdin Madmaati.
Jai Ambe Gauri.

Chand Mund Shonit Beej Hare.
Maiya Shonit Beej Hare
Madhu Kaitabh Doyu Maare Sur Bhayheen Kare.
Jai Ambe Gauri.

Brahmani Rudrani Tum Kamala Rani.
Maiya Tum Kamala Rani
Aagam Nigam Bakhani Tum Shiv Patraani.
Jai Ambe Gauri.

Chausath Yogin Gaavat Nritya Karat Bhairon.
Maiya Nritya Karat Bhairon

Bajat Taal Mridang Aur Bajat Damru.
Jai Ambe Gauri.

Tum Ho Jag Ki Mata Tum Hi Ho Bharta.
Maiya Tum Hi Ho Bharta
Bhaktan Ki Dukh Harta, Sukh Sampatti Karta.
Jai Ambe Gauri.

Bhuja Chaar Ati Shobhit Var Mudra Dhaari.
Maiya Var Mudra Dhaari
Man Wanchhit Phal Paavat Sevat Nar Nari.
Jai Ambe Gauri.

Kanchan Thaal Virajat Agar Kapoor Baati.
Maiya Agar Kapoor Baati
Shreemaalketu Mein Rajat Koti Ratan Jyoti.
Bolo Jai Ambe Gauri.

Maa Ambeji Ki Aarti Jo Koi Nar Gaave.
Maiya Jo Koi Nar Gaave
Kahat Shivanand Swami Sukh Sampatti Paave.
Jai Ambe Gauri.

Devi Vandana

Ya Devi sarvabhuteshu shaktirupena sanstita.

Namastasyai namastasyai namastasyai namo namah.

श्री पार्वती जी की आरती

जय पार्वती माता जय पार्वती माता
ब्रह्मा सनातन देवी शुभफल की दाता ।।

अरिकुलापदम विनाशिनी जय सेवक त्राता,
जगजीवन जगदंबा हरिहर गुणगाता ।।

सिंह को बाहन साजे कुण्डल हैं साथा,
देबबंधु जस गावत नृत्य करा ताथा ।।

सतयुग रूपशील अतिसुन्दर नाम सती कहलाता,
हेमाचल घर जन्मी सखियन संग राता ।।

शुम्भ निशुम्भ विदारे हेमाचल स्थाता,
सहस्त्र भुजा धरिके चक्र लियो हाथा ।।

सृष्टिरूप तुही है जननी शिव संगरंग राता,
नन्दी भृंगी बीन लही है हाथन मद माता ।।

देवन अरज करत तब चित को लाता,
गावन दे दे ताली मन में रंगराता ।।

श्री प्रताप आरती मैया की जो कोई गाता,
सदा सुखी नित रहता सुख सम्पति पाता ।।

Shri Parvati Ji Ki Aarti

Jai Parvati Mata Jai Parvati Mata
Brahma Sanatan Devi Shubhal Phal Ki Data.

Arikulapadam Vinashini Jai Sevak Traata,
Jagjeevan Jagdamba Harihar Gun Gaata.

Sinh Ko Vahan Saaje Kundal Hai Saatha,
Debbandhu Jas Gaavat Nritya Karata Tha.

Satyug Roopshil Atisundar Naam Sati Kahlata,
Hemachal Ghar Janmi Sakhiyan Sang Rata.

Shumbh Nishumbh Vidare Hemachal Sthaata,
Sahastra Bhuja Dhareke Chakra Liya Haatha.

Srishtiroop Tu Hi Hai Janani Shiv Sangrang Rata,
Nandi Bhringi Been Lahi Hai Haathan Mad Mata.

Devan Arj Karat Tab Chit Ko Laata,
Gavan De De Taali Man Mein Rang Rata.

Shri Pratap Aarti Maiya Ki Jo Koi Gaata,
Sada Sukhi Nit Rehta, Sukh Sampatti Paata.

श्री काली माता की आरती

मंगल की सेवा सुन मेरी देवा, हाथ जोड़ तेरे द्वार खड़े।
पान सुपारी ध्वजा नारियल ले ज्वाला तेरी भेट धरेसुन ।।
जगदम्बे न कर विलम्बे, संतन के भडांर भरे।
सन्तन प्रतिपाली सदा खुशहाली, जै काली कल्याण करे ।।
बुद्धि विधाता तू जग माता, मेरा कारज सिद्ध रे।
चरण कमल का लिया आसरा शरण तुम्हारी आन पड़े ।।
जब जब भीड़ पड़ी भक्तन पर, तब तब आप सहाय करे।
गुरु के वार सकल जग मोहयो, तरुणी रूप अनूप धरेमाता ।।
होकर पुत्र खिलावे, कही भार्या भोग करे शुक्र सुखदाई सदा।
सहाई संत खड़े जयकार करे ।।
ब्रह्मा विष्णु महेश फल लिये भेट तेरे द्वार खड़े अटल सिहांसन।
बैठी मेरी माता, सिर सोने का छत्र फिरेवार शनिचर ।।
कुकम बरणो, जब लकड पर हुकुम करे।
खड्ग खप्पर त्रिशुल हाथ लिये, रक्त बीज को भस्म करे ।।
शुम्भ निशुम्भ को क्षण में मारे, महिषासुर को पकड़ दले।
आदित वारी आदि भवानी, जन अपने को कष्ट हरे ।।
कुपित होकर दनव मारे, चण्डमुण्ड सब चूर करे।
जब तुम देखी दया रूप हो, पल मे सकंट दूर करे ।।

सौम्य स्वभाव धरयो मेरी माता, जन की अर्ज कबूल करे।
सात बार की महिमा बरनी, सब गुण कौन बखान करे॥
सिंह पीठ पर चढ़ी भवानी, अटल भवन मे राज्य करे।
दर्शन पावे मंगल गावे, सिद्ध साधक तेरी भेट धरे॥
ब्रह्मा वेद पढ़े तेरे द्वारे, शिव शंकर हरि ध्यान धरे।
इन्द्र कृष्ण तेरी करे आरती, चंवर कुबेर डुलाय रहे॥
जय जननी जय मातु भवानी, अटल भवन मे राज्य करे।
सन्तन प्रतिपाली सदा खुशहाली, मैया जै काली कल्याण करे॥

Shri Kali Mata Ki Aarti

Mangal Ki Seva Sun Meri Deva, Haath Jod Tere Dwaar Khade.

Paan Supari Dhwaja Nariyal Le Jwala Teri Bhet Dhere Sun.

Jagadambe Na Kar Vilambe, Santan Ke Bhandaare Bhare.

Santan Pratipaali Sada Khushhaali, Jai Kali Kalyan Kare.

Buddhi Vidhata Tu Jag Mata, Mera Kaaj Siddh Re.

Charan Kamal Ka Liya Asra, Sharan Tumaari Aan Pade.

Jab Jab Bheed Padi Bhaktan Par, Tab Tab Aap Sahay Kare.

Guru Ke Vaar Sakaal Jag Mohayo, Taruni Roop Anup Dhare Mata.

Hokar Putra Khilaave, Kahi Bharya Bhog Kare

Shukra Sukhdaai Sada,

Sahay Sant Khade Jaaykar Kare.

Brahma Vishnu Mahesh Phal Liye Bhet Tere Dwaar Khade

Atal Singhansan, Baithi Meri Mata, Sir Sone Ka Chhat Firaawar Shanichar.

Kukam Barano, Jab Lakad Par Hukam Kare.

Khadg Khappar Trishul Haath Liye, Rakt Beej Ko Bhasm Kare.

Shumbh Nishumbh Ko Kshan Mein Maare, Mahishasur Ko Pakad Dalae.

Aadit Wari Aadi Bhavani, Jan Apne Ko Kasht Hare.

Kupit Hokar Danuv Maare, Chandmund Sab Choor Kare.

Jab Tum Dekhi Daya Roop Ho, Pal Mein Sankat Door Kare.

Saumy Swabhav Dharayo Meri Mata, Jan Ki Arj Kabool Kare.

Saat Baar Ki Mahima Barni, Sab Gun Kaun Bakhan Kare.

Sinh Peeth Par Chadhi Bhavani, Atal Bhavan Mein Rajya Kare.

Darshan Paave Mangal Gaave, Siddh Saadhak Teri Bhet Dhere.

Brahma Ved Padhe Tere Dware, Shiv Shankar Hari Dhyaan Dhare.

Indra Krishna Teri Kare Aarti, Chavur Kuber Dulaye Rahe.

Jai Janani Jai Matu Bhavani, Atal Bhavan Mein Rajya Kare.

Santan Pratipaali Sada Khushhaali, Maiya Jai Kali Kalyan Kare.

श्री सरस्वती जी की आरती

श्लोकः

या कुन्देन्दुतुषारहारधवला या शुभ्रवस्त्रावृता,
या वीणावरदण्डमण्डितकरा या श्वेतपद्मासना।
या ब्रह्माच्युत शंकरप्रभृतिभिर्देवैः सदा वन्दिता,
सा मां पातु सरस्वती भगवती निःशेषजाड्यापहा ॥
शुक्लां ब्रह्मविचार सार परमामाद्यां जगद्व्यापिनीं,
वीणापुस्तकधारिणीमभयदां जाड्यान्धकारापहाम् ।
हस्ते स्फटिकमालिकां विदधतीं पद्मासने संस्थिताम्,
वन्दे तां परमेश्वरीं भगवतीं बुद्धिप्रदां शारदाम् ॥

जय सरस्वती माता, जय जय हे सरस्वती माता ।
सद्गुण वैभव शालिनी, त्रिभुवन विख्याता ॥
जय सरस्वती माता

चंद्रवदनि पदमासिनी, घुति मंगलकारी ।
सोहें शुभ हंस सवारी, अतुल तेजधारी ॥
जय सरस्वती माता

बायें कर में वीणा, दायें कर में माला।
शीश मुकुट मणी सोहें, गल मोतियन माला॥
जय सरस्वती माता

देवी शरण जो आयें, उनका उद्धार किया।
पैठी मंथरा दासी, रावण संहार किया॥
जय सरस्वती माता

विद्या ज्ञान प्रदायिनी, ज्ञान प्रकाश भरो।
मोह और अज्ञान तिमिर का जग से नाश करो॥
जय सरस्वती माता

धुप, दिप फल मेवा माँ स्वीकार करो।
ज्ञानचक्षु दे माता, भव से उद्धार करो॥
जय सरस्वती माता

माँ सरस्वती जी की आरती जो कोई नर गावें।
हितकारी, सुखकारी ग्यान भक्ती पावें॥
जय सरस्वती माता

सरस्वती माता, जय जय हे सरस्वती माता।
सदगुण वैभव शालिनी, त्रिभुवन विख्याता॥
जय सरस्वती माता

Shri Saraswati Ji Ki Aarti

Shloka:

Ya Kundendu Tushar Har Dhwala, Ya Shubhra Vastra Avrita,
Ya Veena Var Dand Mandit Kara, Ya Shwet Padmaasana.
Ya Brahma Achyut Shankar Prabhritibhih Devaih Sada Vandita,
Sa Maa Patu Saraswati Bhagwati Nisshesh Jadyapaha.
Shuklam Brahma Vichar Sara Paramam Aadyam Jagad Vyapini,
Veena Pustak Dharini Abhayadam, Jadyandhakarapaham.
Haste Sphatik Malikaam Vidadhatiim Padmasane Sansthitaam,
Vande Taam Parameshwari Bhagwatiim Buddhipradam Sharadham.

Jai Saraswati Mata, Jai Jai He Saraswati Mata,
Dagun Vaibhav Shalini, Tribhuvan Vikhyata.
Jai Saraswati Mata.

Chandravadhani Padmasini, Ghuti Mangalkari,
Sohen Shubh Hans Sawari, Atul Tejdhari.
Jai Saraswati Mata.

Baayein Kar Mein Veena, Daayein Kar Mein Mala,
Sheesh Mukut Mani Sohen, Gal Motiyan Mala.
Jai Saraswati Mata.

Devi Sharan Jo Aayein, Unka Uddhar Kiya,
Paithi Manthara Daasi, Ravan Sanhaar Kiya.
Jai Saraswati Mata.

Vidya Gyaan Pradayini, Gyaan Prakash Bharo,
Moh Aur Agyan Timir Ka Jag Se Naash Karo.
Jai Saraswati Mata.

Dhoop, Deep Phal Meva Maa Swikaar Karo,
Gyaan Chashu De Mata, Bhav Se Uddhar Karo.
Jai Saraswati Mata.

Maa Saraswati Ji Ki Aarti Jo Koi Nar Gaave,
Hitkari, Sukhkari, Gyaan Bhakti Paave.
Jai Saraswati Mata.

Saraswati Mata, Jai Jai He Saraswati Mata,
Sadgun Vaibhav Shalini, Tribhuvan Vikhyata.
Jai Saraswati Mata.

श्री लक्ष्मी जी की आरती

श्लोक:

महालक्ष्मी नमस्तुभ्यं, नमस्तुभ्यं सुरेश्वरी।
हरिप्रिये नमस्तुभ्यं, नमस्तुभ्यं दयानिधे ।।

ॐ जय लक्ष्मी माता, मैया जय लक्ष्मी माता।
तुमको निसदिन सेवत, हर विष्णु धाता ।।
ॐ जय लक्ष्मी माता....

उमा, रमा, ब्रम्हाणी, तुम जग की माता।
सूर्य चद्रंमा ध्यावत, नारद ऋषि गाता ।।
ॐ जय लक्ष्मी माता....

दुर्गारूप निरंजनि, सुख संपत्ति दाता।
जो कोई तुमको ध्यावत, ऋद्धि सिद्धि धन पाता ।।
ॐ जय लक्ष्मी माता....

तुम पाताल निवासनी, तुम ही शुभदाता।
कर्मप्रभाव प्रकाशनी, भवनिधि की त्राता ।।
ॐ जय लक्ष्मी माता....

जिस घर तुम रहती, तंह सब सद्गुण आता।
सब सभंव हो जाता, मन नहीं घबराता ।।
ॐ जय लक्ष्मी माता....

तुम बिन यज्ञ ना होता, वस्त्र न कोई पाता ।
खान पान का वैभव, सब तुमसे आता ।।
ॐ जय लक्ष्मी माता....

शुभ गुण मंदिर सुंदर, क्षीरोदधि-जाता।
रत्न चतुर्दश तुम बिन, कोई नहीं पाता ।।
ॐ जय लक्ष्मी माता....

महालक्ष्मी जी की आरती, जो कोई नर गाता ।
उर आंनद समाा, पाप उतर जाता ।।
ॐ जय लक्ष्मी माता....

स्थिर चर जगत बचावै, कर्म प्रेर ल्याता ।
रामप्रताप मैया जी की शुभ दृष्टि पाता ।।
ॐ जय लक्ष्मी माता....

ॐ जय लक्ष्मी माता, मैया जय लक्ष्मी माता ।
तुमको निसदिन सेवत, हर विष्णु धाता ।।
ॐ जय लक्ष्मी माता..

Shri Lakshmi Ji Ki Aarti

Shloka:

Mahalakshmi namasthubhyam, namasthubhyam sureshwari.

Haripriye namasthubhyam, namasthubhyam dayanidhe.

Om Jai Lakshmi Mata, Maiya Jai Lakshmi Mata,
Tumko nis din sevata, Har Vishnu Dhata.
Om Jai Lakshmi Mata...

Uma, Rama, Brahmani, Tum Jag Ki Mata,
Surya Chandrama Dhyavat, Narad Rishi Gata.
Om Jai Lakshmi Mata...

Durga Roop Niranjani, Sukh Sampatti Data,
Jo koi tumko dhyavat, Riddhi Siddhi Dhan Pata.
Om Jai Lakshmi Mata...

Tum patal Nivāsani, Tum hi Shubhdāta,
Karma-prabhav prakāshani, Bhavanidhi ki Trāta.
Om Jai Lakshmi Mata...

Jis ghar tum rahti, Tahm sab sad-gun āta,
Sab sambhav ho jata, Mann nahin ghabrata.
Om Jai Lakshmi Mata...

Tum bin yajña na hota, Vastra na koi pata,
Khan-paan ka vaibhav, sab tumse āta.
Om Jai Lakshmi Mata...

Shubh gun mandir sundar, kshirodadhi jata,
Ratn chaturdasha tum bin, koi nahin pata.
Om Jai Lakshmi Mata...

Mahalakshmi Ji ki Aarti, Jo koi nar gata,
Unhān ānanda samāna, pāp utar jata.
Om Jai Lakshmi Mata...

Sthir char jagat bachawe, karm prērṇā laiyātā,
Rampratāp Maiya Ji ki shubh drishti pāta.
Om Jai Lakshmi Mata...

Om Jai Lakshmi Mata, Maiya Jai Lakshmi Mata,
Tumko nis din sevata, Har Vishnu Vidhata.
Om Jai Lakshmi Mata...

श्री सीता जी की आरती

सीता विराजित मिथिलाधाम, सब मिल कर करें आरती।
संग सुशोभित लछुमन-राम, सब मिल कर करें आरती ।।

विपदा विनाशिनि सुखदा चराचर, सीता धिया बनि आयीं सुनयना घर।
मिथिला के महिमा महान...सब मिल कर करें आरती ।। सीता विराजित ...

सीता सर्वेश्वरि ममता सरोवर, बायाँ कमल कर दायाँ अभय वर।
सौम्या सकल गुणधाम.....सब मिल कर करें आरती ।। सीता विराजित ...

रामप्रिया सर्वमंगल दायिनि, सीता सकल जगती दुःखहारिणि।
करें सबका कल्याण...सब मिल कर करें आरती ।। सीता विराजित ...

सीता-राम की जोड़ी अतिभावन, नैहर सासुर किया पावन
सेवक हैं हनुमान...सब मिल कर करें आरती ।। सीता विराजित ...

ममतामयी माता सीता पुनीता, संतन हेतु सीता सदा सुनीता
धरणी-सुता सब ठाम...सब मिल कर करें आरती ।। सीता विराजित ...

शुक्ल नवमी तिथि वैशाख मासे, 'चंद्रमणि' सीता उत्सव हुलासे
पाय सकल सुखधाम...सब मिल कर करें आरती ।।

सीता विराजित मिथिलाधाम सब मिल कर करें आरती ।।

Shri Sita Ji Ki Aarti

Sita Virajit Mithiladhām, sab mil kar karein Aarti,
Sang Sushobhit Lakshman-Ram, sab mil kar karein Aarti.

Vipada vinashini, Sukhada charachar,
Sita dhiya bani ayi, Sunayana ghar.
Mithila ke Mahima Mahan, sab mil kar karein Aarti.

Sita Sarveshwari, Mamta Sarovar,
Bayan Kamal, Dayan Abhay Var.
Saumya, Sakal Gundham, sab mil kar karein Aarti.

Rampriya Sarvamangaldayani, Sita Sakal Jagati Dukhharini,
Karein sab ka kalyan, sab mil kar karein Aarti.

Sita-Ram ki jodi atibhavan, Naihar Sasur kiya pawan,
Sevak hain Hanuman, sab mil kar karein Aarti.

Mamtamayee Mata Sita Puniya,
Santaan hetu Sita sada suneeta,
Dharani-suta sab tham, sab mil kar karein Aarti.

Shukla Navami Tithi Vaishakh Mas, 'Chandramani' Sita Utsav Hulase,

Pay sakal Sukhadhām, sab mil kar karein Aarti.

Sita Virajit Mithiladhām, sab mil kar karein Aarti.

श्री राधा जी की आरती

आरती श्री वृषभानुसुता की।
मंजु मूर्ति मोहन ममता की॥

त्रिविध तापयुत संसृति नाशिनि,
विमल विवेकविराग विकासिनि।

पावन प्रभु पद प्रीति प्रकाशिनि,
सुन्दरतम छवि सुन्दरता की॥

मुनि मन मोहन मोहन मोहनि,
मधुर मनोहर मूरती सोहनि।

अविरलप्रेम अमिय रस दोहनि,
प्रिय अति सदा सखी ललिताकी॥

संतत सेव्य सत मुनि जनकी,
आकर अमित दिव्यगुन गनकी,

आकर्षिणी कृष्ण तन मनकी,
अति अमूल्य सम्पति समता की ।।

कृष्णात्मिका, कृषण सहचारिणि,
चिन्मयवृन्दा विपिन विहारिणि ।

जगज्जननि जग दु:खनिवारिणि,
आदि अनादिशक्ति विभुताकी ।।

Shri Radha Ji Ki Aarti

Aarti Shri Vrishbhanu Suta Ki
Manju Murti Mohan Mamta Ki.

Trividha Taap Yut Sansriti Naashini,
Vimal Vivek Virag Vikaasini.

Paawan Prabhu Pad Preeti Prakaashini,
Sundartam Chhavi Sundarta Ki.

Muni Man Mohan Mohan Mohani,
Madhur Manohar Moorti Sohani.

Aviral Prem Amrit Ras Dohani,
Priya Ati Sada Sakhi Lalitaki.

Santat Sevy Sat Muni Janaki,
Aakar Amit Divyagun Ganki,

Aakarshini Krishna Tan Manki,
Ati Amulya Sampatti Samta Ki.

Krishnatmika, Krishan Sahcharini,
Chinmayvrinda Vipin Viharini.

Jagat Janani Jag Dukh Nivaarini,
Adi Anadi Shakti Vibhutaki.

श्री संतोषी माता आरती

जय संतोषी माता, मैया जय संतोषी माता।
अपने सेवक जन को, सुख संपति दाता॥

जय सुंदर चीर सुनहरी, मां धारण कीन्हो।
हीरा पन्ना दमके, तन श्रृंगार लीन्हो॥

जय गेरू लाल छटा छवि, बदन कमल सोहे।
मंद हँसत करूणामयी, त्रिभुवन जन मोहे॥

जय स्वर्ण सिंहासन बैठी, चंवर ढुरे प्यारे।
धूप, दीप, मधुमेवा, भोग धरें न्यारे॥

जय गुड़ अरु चना परमप्रिय, तामे संतोष कियो।
संतोषी कहलाई, भक्तन वैभव दियो॥

जय शुक्रवार प्रिय मानत, आज दिवस सोही।
भक्त मण्डली छाई, कथा सुनत मोही॥

जय मंदिर जगमग ज्योति, मंगल ध्वनि छाई।
विनय करें हम बालक, चरनन सिर नाई॥

जय भक्ति भावमय पूजा, अंगीकृत कीजै।
जो मन बसे हमारे, इच्छा फल दीजै॥

जय दुखी, दरिद्री, रोगी, संकटमुक्त किए।
बहु धनधान्य भरे घर, सुख सौभाग्य दिए॥

जय ध्यान धर्यो जिस जन ने, मनवांछित फल पायो।
पूजा कथा श्रवण कर, घर आनंद आयो॥

जय शरण गहे की लज्जा, राखियो जगदंबे।
संकट तू ही निवारे, दयामयी अंबे॥

जय संतोषी मां की आरती, जो कोई नर गावे।
ऋद्धिसिद्धि सुख संपत्ति, जी भरकर पावे॥

Shri Santoshi Mata Ki Aarti

Jai Santoshi Mata, Maiya Jai Santoshi Mata.
Apne Sevak Jan Ko, Sukh Sampatti Daata.

Jai Sundar Cheera Sunahri, Maa Dhaaran Kinho.
Heera Panna Damke, Tan Shringar Leenho.

Jai Geru Laal Chhata Chhavi, Badan Kamal Sohe.
Mand Hansat Karunamayi, Tribhuvan Jan Mohe.

Jai Swarn Singh Asan Baithi, Chamar Dhure Pyare.
Dhoop, Deep, Madhumeva, Bhog Dharen Nyare.

Jai Gud Aru Chana Param Priya, Taame Santoshi Kiyo.
Santoshi Kahlai, Bhaktan Vaibhav Diyo.

Jai Shukravar Priya Maanat, Aaj Divas Sohi.
Bhakt Mandali Chhai, Katha Sunat Mohee.

Jai Mandir Jagmag Jyoti, Mangal Dhwani Chhai.
Vinay Karein Hum Balak, Charan Seer Naai.

Jai Bhakti Bhavmay Pooja, Angikrit Keejai.
Jo Mann Base Hamare, Ichha Phal Deejiye.

Jai Dukhi, Daridri, Rogi, Sankatmukt Kiye.
Bahu Dhan-Dhanya Bhare Ghar, Sukh Saubhagya Diye.

Jai Dhyan Dharyo Jis Jan Ne, Manvanshit Phal Paayo.
Pooja Katha Shravann Kar, Ghar Anand Aayo.

Jai Sharan Gahe Ki Lajja, Rakhiye Jagdambay.
Sankat Tu Hi Nivare, Dayamayi Ambe.

Jai Santoshi Maa Ki Aarti, Jo Koi Nar Gaave.
Riddhi Siddhi Sukh Sampatti, Jee Bhar Ke Paave.

श्री गायत्री माता की आरती

जयति जय गायत्री माता, जयति जय गायत्री माता।

आदि शक्ति तुम अलख निरंजन जग पालन कर्त्री।
दुःख शोक भय क्लेश कलह दारिद्र्य दैन्य हर्त्री ।।१ ।।

ब्रह्मरूपिणी, प्रणत पालिनी, जगत धातृ अम्बे।
भव-भय हारी, जन हितकारी, सुखदा जगदम्बे ।।२ ।।

भयहारिणि, भवतारिणि, अनघे अज आनन्द राशी।
अविकारी, अघहरी, अविचलित, अमले, अविनाशी ।।३ ।।

कामधेनु सत-चित-आनन्दा जय गंगा गीता।
सविता की शाश्वती, शक्ति तुम सावित्री सीता ।।४ ।।

ऋग, यजु, साम, अथर्व, प्रणयिनी, प्रणव महामहिमे।
कुण्डलिनी सहस्रार सुषुम्ना शोभा गुण गरिमे ।।५ ।।

स्वाहा, स्वधा, शची, ब्रह्माणी, राधा, रुद्राणी।
जय सतरूपा वाणी, विद्या, कमला, कल्याणी ।।६ ।।

जननी हम हैं दीन, हीन, दुःख दारिद के घेरे।
यदपि कुटिल, कपटी कपूत तऊ बालक हैं तेरे ।।७ ।।

स्नेह सनी करुणामयि माता चरण शरण दीजै।
बिलख रहे हम शिशु सुत तेरे दया दृष्टि कीजै ।।८ ।।

काम, क्रोध, मद, लोभ, दम्भ, दुर्भाव द्वेष हरिये।
शुद्ध, बुद्धि, निष्पाप हृदय, मन को पवित्र करिये ।।९ ।।

तुम समर्थ सब भाँति तारिणी, तुष्टि, पुष्टि त्राता।
सत मारग पर हमें चलाओ जो है सुखदाता ।।१० ।।

जयति जय गायत्री माता, जयति जय गायत्री माता

Shri Gayatri Mata Ki Aarti

Jayati Jay Gayatri Mata, Jayati Jay Gayatri Mata.

Adi Shakti Tum Alakh Niranjan Jag Paalan Kartari ।
Dukh Shok Bhay Klesh Kalh Daaridrya Dainya Hartri ।।1।।

Brahmarupini, Pranat Paalini, Jagat Dhaatri Ambe ।
Bhav-Bhay Haari, Jan Hitkaari, Sukhda Jagdambe ।।2।।

Bhayhaari, Bhavtaari, Anaghe, Aj Anand Rashi ।
Avikaari, Aghari, Avichalit, Amale, Avinaashi ।।3।।

Kamdhenu Sat-Chit-Anand, Jay Ganga Geeta ।
Savita Ki Shashwati, Shakti Tum Savitri Sita ।।4।।

Rig, Yajur, Saam, Atharv, Pranayini, Pranav Mahamahime ।
Kundalini Sahasraar Sushumra Shobha Gun Garime ।।5।।

Swaha, Swadha, Shachi, Brahmani, Radha, Rudrani ।
Jay Satroopa Vani, Vidya, Kamala, Kalyani ।।6।।

Janani Hum Hai Din, Hin, Dukh Daridr Ke Ghere ।
Yadi Kutil, Kapati Kaput Tahu Baalak Hai Tere ।।7।।

Sneh Sani Karunamayi Mata Charan Sharan Deejiye ।
Bilakh Rahe Hum Shishu Sut Tere Dayaa Drishti Keejiye ।।8।।

Kaam, Krodh, Mad, Lobh, Dambh, Durbhav Dvesh Hariye ।
Shuddh, Buddhi, Nishpaap Hriday, Mann Ko Pavitr Karaye ।।9।।

Tum Samarth Sab Bhaanti Taarini, Tushthi, Pushti Traata ।
Sat Marg Par Humein Chalao Jo Hai Sukhdata ।।10।।

Jayati Jay Gayatri Mata, Jayati Jay Gayatri Mata

श्री अन्नपूर्णा जी की आरती

बारम्बार प्रणाम, मैया बारम्बार प्रणाम...
जो नहीं ध्यावे तुम्हें अम्बिके, कहां उसे विश्राम।
अन्नपूर्णा देवी नाम तिहारो, लेत होत सब काम ।। बारम्बार...

प्रलय युगान्तर और जन्मान्तर, कालान्तर तक नाम।
सुर सुरों की रचना करती, कहाँ कृष्ण कहाँ राम ।। बारम्बार...

चूमहि चरण चतुर चतुरानन, चारु चक्रधर श्याम।
चंद्रचूड़ चन्द्रानन चाकर, शोभा लखहि ललाम ।। बारम्बार...

देवि देव! दयनीय दशा में दया-दया तब नाम।
त्राहि-त्राहि शरणागत वत्सल शरण रूप तब धाम ।। बारम्बार...

श्रीं, ह्रीं श्रद्धा श्रीं ऐं विद्या श्रीं क्लीं कमला काम।
कांति, भ्रांतिमयी, कांति शांतिमयी, वर दे तू निष्काम ।। बारम्बार..

Shri Annapurna Ji Ki Aarti

Barambaar Pranam, Maiya Barambaar Pranam...
Jo Nahin Dhyave Tumhe Ambike, Kahan Use Vishraam.
Annapurna Devi Naam Tiharo, Let Hot Sab Kaam...
Barambaar...

Pralaya Yugantar Aur Janmantar, Kaalantar Tak Naam.
Sur Suron Ki Rachna Karti, Kahan Krishna Kahan Ram...
Barambaar...

Choomahi Charan Chatur Chaturanan, Chaaru Chakradhara Shyam.
Chandrachud Chandranan Chaakar, Shobha Lakhahi Lalaam... Barambaar...

Devi Dev! Dayaneey Dasha Mein Daya-Daya Tab Naam.
Traahi-Traahi Sharanagat Vatsal Sharan Roop Tab Dham...
Barambaar...

Shrim hrim Shraddha, Shrim aim Vidya, Shrim kleem Kamala Kaam.

Kaanti, Bhrantimayi, Kaanti Shantimayi, Var De Tu Nishkaam... Barambaar...

श्री वैष्णो देवी की आरती

जय वैष्णवी माता, मैया जय वैष्णवी माता।
हाथ जोड़ तेरे आगे, आरती मैं गाता ।।

शीश पे छत्र विराजे, मूरतिया प्यारी।
गंगा बहती चरनन, ज्योति जगे न्यारी ।।

ब्रह्मा वेद पढ़े नित द्वारे, शंकर ध्यान धरे।
सेवक चंवर डुलावत, नारद नृत्य करे ।।

सुन्दर गुफा तुम्हारी, मन को अति भावे।
बार-बार देखन को, ऐ माँ मन चावे ।।

भवन पे झण्डे झूलें, घंटा ध्वनि बाजे।
ऊँचा पर्वत तेरा, माता प्रिय लागे ।।

पान सुपारी ध्वजा नारियल, भेंट पुष्प मेवा।
दास खड़े चरणों में, दर्शन दो देवा ।।

जो जन निश्चय करके, द्वार तेरे आवे।
उसकी इच्छा पूरण, माता हो जावे ।।

इतनी स्तुति निश-दिन, जो नर भी गावे।
कहते सेवक ध्यानू, सुख सम्पत्ति पावे

Shri Vaishno Devi Ki Aarti

Jai Vaishnavi Mata, Maiya Jai Vaishnavi Mata.
Haath Jod Tere Aage, Aarti Main Gata.

Sheesh Pe Chhat Viraje, Moorti Pyari.
Ganga Baheti Charan, Jyoti Jage Nyari.

Brahma Ved Padhe Nit Dware, Shankar Dhyaan Dhare.
Sevak Chamar Dulawat, Narad Nritya Kare.

Sundar Gufa Tumhari, Mann Ko Ati Bhaave.
Bar-Bar Dekhan Ko, Ai Maa Mann Chaave.

Bhawan Pe Jhandey Jhule, Ghanta Dhvani Baaje.
Ooncha Parvat Tera, Mata Priya Laage.

Paan Supari Dhwaja Nariyal, Bhent Pushp Meva.
Daas Khade Charano Mein, Darshan Do Deva.

Jo Jan Nischay Karke, Dwaar Tere Aave.
Uski Ichha Pooran, Mata Ho Jaave.

Itni Stuti Nish-Din, Jo Nar Bhi Gaave.
Kahte Sevak Dhyanu, Sukh Sampatti Paave.

श्री तुलसी जी की आरती

जय जय तुलसी माता, सबकी सुखदाता वर माता।
सब योगों के ऊपर, सब रोगों के ऊपर,
रुज से रक्षा करके भव त्राता।
जय जय तुलसी माता।

बहु पुत्री है श्यामा, सूर वल्ली है ग्राम्या,
विष्णु प्रिय जो तुमको सेवे, सो नर तर जाता।
जय जय तुलसी माता।

हरि के शीश विराजत त्रिभुवन से हो वंदित,
पतित जनों की तारिणि, तुम हो विख्याता।
जय जय तुलसी माता।

लेकर जन्म बिजन में आई दिव्य भवन में,
मानव लोक तुम्हीं से सुख सम्पत्ति पाता।
जय जय तुलसी माता।

हरि को तुम अति प्यारी श्याम वर्ण सुकुमारी,
प्रेम अजब है श्री हरि का तुम से नाता।
जय जय तुलसी माता

Shri Tulsi Ji Ki Aarti

Jai Jai Tulsi Mata, Sabki Sukhdata Var Mata.
Sab Yogon Ke Upar, Sab Rogon Ke Upar,
Ruj Se Raksha Karke Bhav Traata.
Jai Jai Tulsi Mata.

Bahut Putri Hai Shyama, Sur Vallabh Hai Gramiya,
Vishnu Priya Jo Tumko Seve, So Nar Tar Jaata.
Jai Jai Tulsi Mata.

Hari Ke Sheesh Virajat Tribhuvan Se Ho Vandit,
Patit Jano Ki Taarini, Tum Ho Vikhyaata.
Jai Jai Tulsi Mata.

Leker Janm Bijan Mein Aayi Divya Bhavan Mein,
Manav Lok Tumhi Se Sukh Sampatti Paata.
Jai Jai Tulsi Mata.

Hari Ko Tum Ati Pyari Shyam Varn Sukumari,
Prem Ajab Hai Shri Hari Ka Tum Se Naata.
Jai Jai Tulsi Mata.

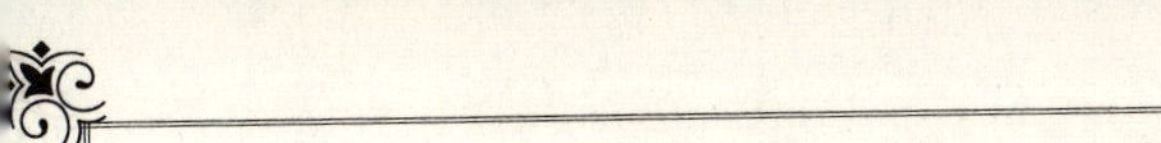

श्री गंगा जी की आरती

ॐ जय गंगे माता, मैया जय गंगे माता।
जो नर तुमको ध्याता, मनवांछित फल पाता ।।
ॐ जय गंगे माता ।।

चन्द्र-सी ज्योति तुम्हारी, जल निर्मल आता।
शरण पड़े जो तेरी, सो नर तर जाता ।।
ॐ जय गंगे माता ।।

पुत्र सगर के तारे, सब जग को ज्ञाता।
कृपा दृष्टि हो तुम्हारी, त्रिभुवन सुख दाता ।।
ॐ जय गंगे माता ।।

एक बार जो प्राणी, शरण तेरी आता।
यम की त्रास मिटाकर, परमगति पाता ।।
ॐ जय गंगे माता ।।

आरती मातु तुम्हारी, जो नर नित गाता।
सेवक वही सहज में, मुक्ति को पाता ।।
ॐ जय गंगे माता

Shri Ganga Ji Ki Aarti

Om Jai Gange Mata, Maiya Jai Gange Mata.
Jo Nar Tumko Dhyata, Manvanshit Phal Paata.
Om Jai Gange Mata.

Chandra-Se Jyoti Tumhari, Jal Nirmal Aata.
Sharan Pade Jo Teri, So Nar Tar Jaata.
Om Jai Gange Mata.

Putra Sagar Ke Taare, Sab Jag Ko Jhaata.
Kripa Drishti Ho Tumhari, Tribhuwan Sukh Data.
Om Jai Gange Mata.

Ek Baar Jo Paani, Sharan Teri Aata.
Yam Ki Tiraas Mitakar, Parmagati Paata.
Om Jai Gange Mata.

Aarti Maat Tumhari, Jo Nar Nit Gaata.
Sevak Wahi Sahaj Mein, Mukti Ko Paata.
Om Jai Gange Mata.

श्री ललिता माता की आरती

श्री मातेश्वरी जय त्रिपुरेश्वरी।
राजेश्वरी जय नमो नमः ।।
करुणामयी सकल अघ हारिणी।
अमृत वर्षिणी नमो नमः ।।
जय शरणं वरणं नमो नमः।
श्री मातेश्वरी जय त्रिपुरेश्वरी ।।
अशुभ विनाशिनी, सब सुख दायिनी।
खल-दल नाशिनी नमो नमः ।।
भण्डासुर वधकारिणी जय माँ।
करुणा कलिते नमो नमः ।।
जय शरणं वरणं नमो नमः।
श्री मातेश्वरी जय त्रिपुरेश्वरी ।।
भव भय हारिणी, कष्ट निवारिणी।
शरण गति दो नमो नमः ।।
शिव भामिनी साधक मन हारिणी।
आदि शक्ति जय नमो नमः ।।
जय शरणं वरणं नमो नमः।
जय त्रिपुर सुन्दरी नमो नमः ।।
श्री मातेश्वरी जय त्रिपुरेश्वरी।
राजेश्वरी जय नमो नमः

Shri Lalita Mata Ki Aarti

Shri Mateshwari Jai Tripureshwari,
Rajeshwari Jai Namo Namah.
Karunamayi Sakal Agh Harini,
Amrit Varshini Namo Namah.
Jai Sharanam Varanam Namo Namah,
Shri Mateshwari Jai Tripureshwari.
Ashubh Vinashini, Sab Sukh Dayini,
Khal-Dal Nashini Namo Namah.
Bhandasur Vadhkarini Jai Maa,
Karuna Kalite Namo Namah.
Jai Sharanam Varanam Namo Namah,
Shri Mateshwari Jai Tripureshwari.
Bhav Bhay Harini, Kasht Nivaarini,
Sharan Gati Do Namo Namah.
Shiv Bhamini Sadhak Man Harini,
Adi Shakti Jai Namo Namah.
Jai Sharanam Varanam Namo Namah,
Jai Tripur Sundari Namo Namah.
Shri Mateshwari Jai Tripureshwari,
Rajeshwari Jai Namo Namah.

श्री एकादशी माता की आरती

ॐ जय एकादशी, जय एकादशी, जय एकादशी माता।
विष्णु पूजा व्रत को धारण कर, शक्ति मुक्ति पाता।।
ॐ जय एकादशी... ।।

तेरे नाम गिनाऊं देवी, भक्ति प्रदान करनी।
गण गौरव की देनी माता, शास्त्रों में वरनी।।
ॐ जय एकादशी... ।।

मार्गशीर्ष के कृष्णपक्ष की उत्पन्ना, विश्वतारनी जन्मी।
शुक्ल पक्ष में हुई मोक्षदा, मुक्तिदाता बन आई।।
ॐ जय एकादशी... ।।

पौष के कृष्णपक्ष की, सफला नामक है।
शुक्लपक्ष में होय पुत्रदा, आनन्द अधिक रहै।।
ॐ जय एकादशी... ।।

नाम षटतिला माघ मास में, कृष्णपक्ष आवै।
शुक्लपक्ष में जया, कहावै, विजय सदा पावै।।
ॐ जय एकादशी... ।।

विजया फागुन कृष्णपक्ष में शुक्ला आमलकी।
पापमोचनी कृष्ण पक्ष में, चौत्र महाबलि की।।
ॐ जय एकादशी... ।।

चैत्र शुक्ल में नाम कामदा, धन देने वाली।
नाम बरुथिनी कृष्णपक्ष में, वैसाख माह वाली।।
ॐ जय एकादशी... ।।

शुक्ल पक्ष में होय मोहिनी अपरा ज्येष्ठ कृष्णपक्षी।
नाम निर्जला सब सुख करनी, शुक्लपक्ष रखी।।
ॐ जय एकादशी... ।।

योगिनी नाम आषाढ़ में जानों, कृष्णपक्ष करनी।
देवशयनी नाम कहायो, शुक्लपक्ष धरनी।।
ॐ जय एकादशी... ।।

कामिका श्रावण मास में आवै, कृष्णपक्ष कहिए।
श्रावण शुक्ला होय पवित्रा आनन्द से रहिए।।
ॐ जय एकादशी... ।।

अजा भाद्रपद कृष्णपक्ष की, परिवर्तिनी शुक्ला।
इन्द्रा आश्चिन कृष्णपक्ष में, व्रत से भवसागर निकला।।
ॐ जय एकादशी... ।।

पापांकुशा है शुक्ल पक्ष में, आप हरनहारी।
रमा मास कार्तिक में आवै, सुखदायक भारी।।
ॐ जय एकादशी... ।।

देवोत्थानी शुक्लपक्ष की, दुखनाशक मैया।
पावन मास में करूं विनती पार करो नैया।।
ॐ जय एकादशी... ।।

परमा कृष्णपक्ष में होती, जन मंगल करनी।
शुक्ल मास में होय पद्मिनी दुख दारिद्र हरनी।।
ॐ जय एकादशी... ।।

जो कोई आरती एकादशी की, भक्ति सहित गावै।
जन गुरदिता स्वर्ग का वासा, निश्चय वह पावै।।
ॐ जय एकादशी...

Shri Ekadashi Mata Ki Aarti

Om Jai Ekadashi, Jai Ekadashi, Jai Ekadashi Mata.
Vishnu Pooja Vrat Ko Dharan Kar, Shakti Mukti Paata.
Om Jai Ekadashi...

Tere Naam Ginaoon Devi, Bhakti Pradan Karni.
Gan Gaurav Ki Deni Mata, Shastron Mein Varni.
Om Jai Ekadashi...

Margashirsha Ke Krishnapaksha Ki Utpanna, Vishwataarni Janmi.
Shukla Paksha Mein Hui Mokshda, Muktidata Ban Aayi.
Om Jai Ekadashi...

Paush Ke Krishnapaksha Ki, Saphala Namak Hai.
Shuklapaksha Mein Hoy Putrada, Anand Adhik Rahe.
Om Jai Ekadashi...

Naam Shattila Magh Maas Mein, Krishnapaksha Aave.
Shuklapaksha Mein Jaya, Kahave, Vijay Sada Paave.
Om Jai Ekadashi...

Vijaya Phagun Krishnapaksha Mein Shukla Aamlaaki.

Paapmochani Krishnapaksha Mein, Chaitra Mahabali Ki.

Om Jai Ekadashi...

Chaitra Shukla Mein Naam Kamda, Dhan Dene Wali.

Naam Baruthini Krishnapaksha Mein, Vaishakh Maah Wali.

Om Jai Ekadashi...

Shukla Paksha Mein Hoy Mohini Apara Jyeshtha Krishnapakshi.

Naam Nirjala Sab Sukh Karni, Shuklapaksha Rakhi.

Om Jai Ekadashi...

Yogini Naam Ashadh Mein Jano, Krishnapaksha Karni.

Devshayani Naam Kahayo, Shuklapaksha Dharani.

Om Jai Ekadashi...

Kamika Shravan Maas Mein Aave, Krishnapaksha Kahin.

Shravan Shukla Hoy Pavitra Anand Se Rahiye.

Om Jai Ekadashi...

Aja Bhadrapad Krishnapaksha Ki, Parivartini Shukla.
Indra Ashchhin Krishnapaksha Mein, Vrat Se Bhavasagar Nikla.
Om Jai Ekadashi...

Paapankusha Hai Shukla Paksha Mein, Aap Haranhari.
Rama Maas Kartik Mein Aave, Sukhdayak Bhari.
Om Jai Ekadashi...

Devuthani Shuklapaksha Ki, Dukh Nashak Maiya.
Pavan Maas Mein Karoon Vinati, Paar Karo Naiya.
Om Jai Ekadashi...

Parma Krishnapaksha Mein Hoti, Jan Mangal Karni.
Shukla Maas Mein Hoy Padmini, Dukh Daridra Harni.
Om Jai Ekadashi...

Jo Koi Aarti Ekadashi Ki, Bhakti Sahit Gaave.
Jan Gurdita Swarg Ka Vasa, Nishchay Wah Paave.
Om Jai Ekadashi...

श्री रामायण जी की आरती

आरती श्री रामायण जी की।
कीरति कलित ललित सिया-पी की ।।
गावत ब्राह्मादिक मुनि नारद। बाल्मीकि विज्ञान विशारद।
शुक सनकादि शेष अरु शारद। बरनि पवनसुत कीरति नीकी ।।
आरती श्री रामायण जी की।

कीरति कलित ललित सिया-पी की ।।
गावत वेद पुरान अष्टदस। छओं शास्त्र सब ग्रन्थन को रस।
मुनि-मन धन सन्तन को सरबस। सार अंश सम्मत सबही की ।।
आरती श्री रामायण जी की।

कीरति कलित ललित सिया-पी की ।।
गावत सन्तत शम्भू भवानी। अरु घट सम्भव मुनि विज्ञानी।
व्यास आदि कविबर्ज बखानी। कागभुषुण्डि गरुड़ के ही की ।।
आरती श्री रामायण जी की।

कीरति कलित ललित सिया-पी की ॥

कलिमल हरनि विषय रस फीकी। सुभग सिंगार मुक्ति जुबती की।

दलन रोग भव मूरि अमी की। तात मात सब विधि तुलसी की ॥

आरती श्री रामायण जी की।

कीरति कलित ललित सिया-पी की ॥

Shri Ramayan Ji Ki Aarti

Aarti Shri Ramayan Ji Ki,
Kirti Kalit Lalit Siya-Pi Ki.
Gavat Brahmadik Muni Narad,
Balmiki Vigyan Visharad.
Shuk Sanakadi Shesh Aru Sharad,
Barni Pavan-Sut Kirti Neeki.
Aarti Shri Ramayan Ji Ki,

Kirti Kalit Lalit Siya-Pi Ki.
Gavat Ved Puran Ashtadas,
Chhao Shastra Sab Granthon Ko Ras.
Muni-Man Dhan Santan Ko Sarbas,
Saar Ansh Sammath Sabhi Ki.
Aarti Shri Ramayan Ji Ki,

Kirti Kalit Lalit Siya-Pi Ki.
Gavat Santat Shambhu Bhavani,
Aru Ghat Sambhav Muni Vigyani.
Vyas Aadi Kavibharj Bakhaani,

Kaagbhushundi Garud Ke Hi Ki.

Aarti Shri Ramayan Ji Ki,

Kirti Kalit Lalit Siya-Pi Ki.

Kalimala Harani Vishay Ras Feeki,

Subhag Singar Mukti Jubati Ki.

Dalan Rog Bhav Moora Ami Ki,

Taat Maat Sab Vidhi Tulsiki.

Aarti Shri Ramayan Ji Ki,

Kirti Kalit Lalit Siya-Pi Ki.

श्री खाटू श्याम आरती

ॐ जय श्री श्याम हरे,
बाबा जय श्री श्याम हरे।
खाटू धाम विराजत,
अनुपम रूप धरे।।
ॐ जय श्री श्याम हरे,
बाबा जय श्री श्याम हरे।

रतन जड़ित सिंहासन,
सिर पर चंवर ढुरे।
तन केसरिया बागो,
कुण्डल श्रवण पड़े।।
ॐ जय श्री श्याम हरे,
बाबा जय श्री श्याम हरे।

गल पुष्पों की माला,
सिर पार मुकुट धरे।
खेवत धूप अग्नि पर,
दीपक ज्योति जले।।
ॐ जय श्री श्याम हरे,
बाबा जय श्री श्याम हरे।

मोदक खीर चूरमा,
सुवरण थाल भरे।
सेवक भोग लगावत,
सेवा नित्य करे।।
ॐ जय श्री श्याम हरे,
बाबा जय श्री श्याम हरे।

झांझ कटोरा और घडियावल,
शंख मृदंग घुरे।
भक्त आरती गावे,
जय-जयकार करे।।
ॐ जय श्री श्याम हरे,
बाबा जय श्री श्याम हरे।

जो ध्यावे फल पावे,
सब दुःख से उबरे।
सेवक जन निज मुख से,
श्री श्याम-श्याम उचरे।।
ॐ जय श्री श्याम हरे,
बाबा जय श्री श्याम हरे।

श्री श्याम बिहारी जी की आरती,
जो कोई नर गावे।
कहत भक्त-जन,
मनवांछित फल पावे।।
ॐ जय श्री श्याम हरे,
बाबा जय श्री श्याम हरे।

जय श्री श्याम हरे,
बाबा जी श्री श्याम हरे।
निज भक्तों के तुमने,
पूरण काज करे।।
ॐ जय श्री श्याम हरे,
बाबा जय श्री श्याम हरे।

ॐ जय श्री श्याम हरे,
बाबा जय श्री श्याम हरे।
खाटू धाम विराजत,
अनुपम रूप धरे।।
ॐ जय श्री श्याम हरे,
बाबा जय श्री श्याम हरे।

श्री श्याम विनती: हाथ जोड़ विनती
करू तो सुनियो चित्त लगाये!

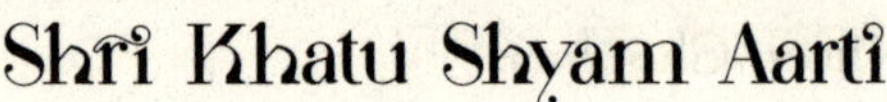

Shri Khatu Shyam Aarti

Om Jai Shri Shyam Hare,
Baba Jai Shri Shyam Hare.
Khatu Dham Birajat,
Anupam Roop Dhare.
Om Jai Shri Shyam Hare,
Baba Jai Shri Shyam Hare.

Ratan Jadit Singhasan,
Sar per Chanvar Dhule.
Tan Kehariya Bago,
Kundal Shravan Pade.
Om Jai Shri Shyam Hare,
Baba Jai Shri Shyam Hare.

Gal Pushpon Ki Maala,
Sir per Mukut Dhare.
Khevat Dhoop, Agni Par,
Deepak Jyoti Jale.
Om Jai Shri Shyam Hare,
Baba Jai Shri Shyam Hare.

Modak, Kheer, Choorma,
Suvaran Thaal Bhare.
Seval Bhog Lagavat,
Seva Nitya Kare.
Om Jai Shri Shyam Hare,
Baba Jai Shri Shyam Hare.

Jhanj, Katora Aur Ghadiyaval,
Shankh Mridang Ghure.
Bhakt Aarti Gaave,
Jai Jaikar Kare.
Om Jai Shri Shyam Hare,
Baba Jai Shri Shyam Hare.

Jo Dhyave Fal Paave,
Sab Dukh Se Ubre.
Sevak Jan Nij Mukhse,
Shri Shyam Shyam Uchre.
Om Jai Shri Shyam Hare,
Baba Jai Shri Shyam Hare.

Shri Shyam Bihariji Ki Aarti,
Jo Koi Nar Gaave.

Kehat Sudhir Agyaani,
Manvanchit Fal Paave.
Om Jai Shri Shyam Hare,
Baba Jai Shri Shyam Hare.

Om Jai Shri Shyam Hare,
Baba Jai Shri Shyam Hare,
Nij Bhaktom Ke Tumne,
Pooran Kaaj Kare.

Om Jai Shri Shyam Hare,
Baba Jai Shri Shyam Hare.
Khatu Dham Birajat,
Anupam Roop Dhare.
Om Jai Shri Shyam Hare....

Shyam Puspanjali Shri Khatu Shyamji Vinat